FUNNY JOKES

FOR

10

YEAR OLD KIDS

HUNDREDS OF HILARIOUS JOKES INSIDE!

JIMMY JONES

Hundreds of really funny, hilarious jokes that will have the kids in fits of laughter in no time!

They're all in here - the funniest
- Jokes
- Riddles
- Tongue Twisters
- Knock Knock Jokes

for 10 year old kids!

Funny kids love funny jokes and this brand new collection of original and classic jokes promises hours of fun for the whole family!

Books by Jimmy Jones

Funny Jokes For Funny Kids
Knock Knock Jokes For Funny Kids

Funny Jokes For Kids Series
All Ages 5 -12!

To see all the latest books by
Jimmy Jones just go to
kidsjokebooks.com

Contents

Funny Jokes!

What did the doctor say to the patient who thought he was an alligator?

Snap out of it!

How did the dinosaur find his wife?

Carbon dating!

If a butcher is 5 feet tall and has big feet what does he weigh?

Meat!

What do you call a girl who likes to cook outside?

Barbie!

What do you call 5 security guards at the Samsung shop?

Guardians of the Galaxy!

What do you have if an elephant sits on your friend?

A flat mate!

Why did the baker quit making doughnuts?
He was just sick of the hole thing!

Why did the 3 scientists get rid of their doorbell?
So they could win the no-bell prize!

What are 2 birds in love called?
Tweet hearts!

What do you call a vampire Santa Claus?
Sackula!

What do lamps wear on a sunny day?
Shades!

What did the doctor say to the patient who thought he was a cat?
How are the kittens?

Why did Mickey Mouse join NASA?
He wanted to visit Pluto!

Why are writers good at writing?
They have a lot of comma sense!

Why did the racehorse go to the drive through?
He wanted some fast food!

Which insect can tell the time?
A Clock-roach!

Why did the chemistry teacher keep on telling jokes?
He was getting a good reaction!

What do you call a boy with no money?
Nickel-less! (Nicholas)

Why did the crocodile buy a GPS?
To be a navi-Gator!

What did the big raindrop say to the small raindrop?
Two's company but three's a cloud!

What happened to the plastic surgeon when he sat too close to the fire?
He melted!

Which fish has the loudest laugh?
A piran-ha-ha-ha!

Why was the farmer bad at telling jokes?
They were too corny!

Why did the chicken cross the playground?
To get to the other slide!

What was the snake's favorite subject at snake school?

Hiss-story!

Why did the computer wear glasses?

To improve its web sight!

Why did the giant squid eat six ships that were carrying potatoes?

Nobody can only eat one potato ship!

Why did the football coach go to the bank before the big game?

To get his quarterback!

Why did the cows all go to Broadway?

To see the mooosicals!

What do you call a bruise on a T-Rex's leg?

A Dino Sore!

Why did Johnny bring a ladder to his school?

So he could go to high school!

Why didn't the skeleton play church music?

He had no organs!

Which dinosaur played golf?

The Tee Rex!

How do fleas get to the next town?
They catch a dog!

What shoes do ninjas wear?
Sneakers!

Why shouldn't dogs eat clocks?
They get ticks!

What is the name of the cat that lives at the hospital?
First aid kit!

Why is it so expensive to have pet pelicans?
You get huge bills!

What is a skunk's favorite Christmas song?
Jingle smells, jingle smells!

What is worse than finding a worm when you are eating an apple?

Finding half the worm!

Why can cows speak to ghosts?

They are on the udder side!

What does a frog like to drink with his dinner?

Croak-a-cola!

Why did the farmer slap the haystack?
It was time to hit the hay!

What do fish like to watch on TV?
Whale of Fortune!

What do dogs love to eat for breakfast?
Pooched eggs!

What do you call a boy named Lee sitting by himself?

Lonely! (Lone Lee)

Which musical instrument is in your bathroom?

The tuba toothpaste!

Why did the mom serve hay for dinner?

Her son could eat like a horse!

Why did the astronaut leave the crowded room?

He needed some space!

How do you know if a hippo has been living in your refrigerator?

There are footprints in the butter!

Why did the flea lose his job?

He wasn't up to scratch!

What did the dinosaur eat after his tooth was pulled out?

The dentist!

What dance to astronauts do?

The moon walk!

Why did the weatherman leave the studio?

The newsreader stole his thunder!

When it gets really cold what does an octopus wear?

His coat of arms!

What do you call your dad when he is covered in snow?

Pop-sicle!

What do you call a hippo with a messy room?

A Hippopota Mess!

How did the barber win the marathon?
He took a shortcut!

What is another name for a cowboy fish?
Billy the squid!

What did the jar of paste say on January 1?
Happy Glue Year!

What is an alligator's favorite sports drink?
GatorAde!

What is a superhero's favorite cereal?
Iron Bran!

Why did the pony stop singing in the farm band?
She was a little hoarse!

Why did the robber lift weights at the gym?
To have buns of steal!

What glasses do really small insects wear?
Speck-tacles!

How do ghosts get their mail?
From the ghost office!

What is a Lion with no eyes called?
Lon!

Why didn't the girl like the pizza joke?
It was way too cheesy!

What did the baby corn ask his mother?
Where is pop corn?

Why did the dentist get promoted?
She knew the drill!

What did the fish name his son?
Gill!

What did the doctor say to the lady whose son swallowed a bullet?
Don't point him at me!

Why didn't the girl change the goldfishes water?

The goldfish hadn't drunk it all yet!

When the buffalo was leaving to go to work, what did he say to his son?

Bison! (bye son!)

Which dinosaur can spin around really quickly on one leg?

The Tricera-tops!

Why was the vampire in the circus?
To be an acro-bat!

Why did the whale get dressed in his best clothes?
He was going to the Orca-stra!

Why couldn't the astronaut go to the moon?
It was full!

What happens if you read lots of books on a hot day at the beach?

You are well red!

Why did the monkey eat 12 bananas?

He found them very a-peeling!

How can you tell if a vampire is getting a cold?

By his loud coffin!

Why did the chicken join the band?
She already had the drumsticks!

How did the wrinkled dress feel?
De-pressed!

Why couldn't the beaver check his email?
He didn't log in!

Why do basketball players love babies so much?

Because they both dribble!

Why was the computer feeling so cold?

It's Windows were left open!

How do owls send messages around the forest?

By tree mail!

Funny Knock Knock Jokes!

Knock knock.

Who's there?

Harley.

Harley who?

Harley ever see you nowadays! How are the kids?

Knock knock.

Who's there?

Beth.

Beth who?

Beth friends stick together so let's go!

Knock knock.

Who's there?

Howie.

Howie who?

Howie going to get there on time?

I know. Let's run!

Knock knock.

Who's there?

Arthur.

Arthur who?

Arthur any leftovers from lunch?

I'm really hungry!

Knock knock.

Who's there?

Quacker.

Quacker who?

Quacker another funny joke!

I love them!

Knock knock.

Who's there?

Cash.

Cash who?

Actually I prefer peanuts mixed with almonds!

Knock knock.

Who's there?

Irish.

Irish who?

Irish I was taller.

Then I could reach the doorbell!

Knock knock.

Who's there?

Ray.

Ray who?

Ray member when we first met?

Love at first sight!

Knock knock.

Who's there?

Carla.

Carla who?

Can you Carla taxi for me please?

Thank you so much!

Knock knock.

Who's there?

Dora.

Dora who?

Dora's locked so should I climb

through the window?

Knock knock.

Who's there?

Bruce.

Bruce who?

I have a Bruce on my leg from when I fell over!

Knock knock.

Who's there?

Elsa.

Elsa who?

Who Elsa do you think it would be?

Let me in!

Knock knock.

Who's there?

Miles.

Miles who?

I walked Miles to get here!

I'm glad you're home!

Knock knock.

Who's there?

Hippo.

Hippo who?

Hippo birthday to you!

Hippo birthday to you!

Knock knock.

Who's there?

Herd.

Herd who?

I herd you were home!

Why didn't you call?

Knock knock.

Who's there?

Snow.

Snow who?

Snow use asking me! I'm 100 years

old and can't remember a thing!

Knock knock.

Who's there?

Norway.

Norway who?

That's Norway to talk to a friend!

Knock knock.

Who's there?

Monacles.

Monacles who?

Monacles are sore from so much knocking. I think I need a band aid!

Knock knock.

Who's there?

Dismay.

Dismay who?

Dismay be the last time I ever knock!

Knock knock.

Who's there?

Sir.

Sir who?

Sir prise! I bet you weren't expecting me, were you?

Knock knock.

Who's there?

Gwen.

Gwen who?

Gwen you have finished your homework, let's go fishing!

Knock knock.

Who's there?

Amma.

Amma who?

Amma not going to tell you until you open this door!

Knock knock.

Who's there?

Canoe.

Canoe who?

Canoe come outside to play?

Knock knock.

Who's there?

Claire.

Claire who?

Claire the way! I need to use the bathroom! Quickly!

Knock knock.

Who's there?

Fixture.

Fixture who?

Fixture doorbell. That will be $100 thank you!

Knock knock.

Who's there?

Phone.

Phone who?

Phonely I had known you were home I would have knocked earlier!

Knock knock.

Who's there?

Quack.

Quack who?

These jokes totally quack me up!

Shall we read them all again?

Knock knock.

Who's there?

Des.

Des who?

Des no way I can reach the bell! Help!

Knock knock.

Who's there?

Aisle.

Aisle who?

Aisle be over at Jack's place if you need me!

Knock knock.

Who's there?

Window.

Window who?

Window you have time to come over to my house?

Knock knock.

Who's there?

Hada.

Hada who?

Hada great weekend, how about you?

Knock knock.

Who's there?

Wilma.

Wilma who?

Wilma key ever work on this door!

Knock knock.

Who's there?

Althea.

Althea who?

Althea later on, dude!

Knock knock.

Who's there?

Barbie.

Barbie who?

Barbie Q Chicken for dinner?

Yummy!

Knock knock.

Who's there?

Boo.

Boo who?

It's not that sad!

Pull yourself together!

Knock knock.

Who's there?

Hacienda.

Hacienda who?

Hacienda the story! Time for bed!

Knock knock.

Who's there?

Howard.

Howard who?

Howard I know what Howard's last name is? I only just met him!

Knock knock.

Who's there?

Radio.

Radio who?

Radio not, I'm coming in!

Knock knock.

Who's there?

Justin.

Justin who?

Justin time for dinner! Smells good!

Knock knock.

Who's there?

Russian.

Russian who?

I'm Russian to get to school! Let's go!

Knock knock.

Who's there?

Bed.

Bed who?

Bed you I can run faster than you.

Ready, set, GO!!

Knock knock.

Who's there?

Spell.

Spell who?

OK W. H. O.

Knock knock.

Who's there?

Patrick.

Patrick who?

Patricked me into knocking on your door! Sorry!

Knock knock.

Who's there?

Iva.

Iva who?

Iva feeling we have met before somewhere!

Knock knock.

Who's there?

Wire.

Wire who?

Wire you still inside? Let's go!

Knock knock.

Who's there?

Whale.

Whale who?

Please wait here a whale. I'll be back in a minute!

Knock knock.

Who's there?

Thumping.

Thumping who?

Thumping grey and thlimy is crawling up your leg!

Knock knock.

Who's there?

Barbara.

Barbara who?

Barbara black sheep, have you any wool?

Knock knock.

Who's there?

Peas.

Peas who?

Peas let me in! I really need to use the bathroom! It's an emergency!

Knock knock.

Who's there?

Doughnut.

Doughnut who?

I doughnut know! I forgot my name!

Knock knock.

Who's there?

Cheese.

Cheese who?

Cheese a very good singer. Want to see her new band?

Knock knock.

Who's there?

Butternut.

Butternut who?

Butternut be late! Let's go right now!

Knock knock.

Who's there?

Comb.

Comb who?

Comb outside and I will tell you!

Knock knock.

Who's there?

Figs.

Figs who?

Figs the doorbell please. All this knocking hurts me hand!

Knock knock.

Who's there?

Harmony.

Harmony who?

Harmony times do I have to knock?

Please answer the door!

Knock knock.

Who's there?

Keanu.

Keanu who?

Keanu open this door before I freeze

to death!

Knock knock.

Who's there?

Amarillo.

Amarillo who?

Amarillo nice guy! Just ask me!

Knock knock.

Who's there?

Frankfurter.

Frankfurter who?

Frankfurter lovely evening!

Knock knock.

Who's there?

Wooden Shoe.

Wooden shoe who?

Wooden shoe know it! Grandma

finally got her driving licence!

Knock knock.

Who's there?

Bacon.

Bacon who?

I'm bacon a cake for your birthday!

Do you want chocolate or fruit cake?

Funny Riddles!

What has many keys but can't open a door?
A piano!

What allows you to look straight through walls?
A window!

What is a Dalmatian's favorite dessert?
Pup-cakes!

How can you spell 'mouse trap' with only 3 letters?

C A T!

What has feet on the inside but not the outside?

Shoes!

If you had lots and lots of different animals together, what would they eat?

Zoo-chini!

What is dirty after washing?
The bath water!

What is the best drink to have in art class?
Crayon-berry!

What do you call books on the very top shelf in the library?
Tall tales!

What is at the end of the rainbow?
The letter W!

What falls in winter but never gets hurt?
Snow!

Which animal can fix leaky taps?
A seal!

What kind of bow is very hard to tie?
A rainbow!

How could the man who shaved many times
a day still have a beard?
He was a barber!

Who never needs to iron any clothes?
The Wash and Wear Wolf!

What can you catch but never throw?
A cold!

Which cheese is made backwards?
Edam!

What do crocodiles use in math class?
A Calcu-gator!

What do pirates eat for dinner?
Pizzas of eight!

What has fingers and a thumb but no arm?
A glove!

What do you call false teeth in the White House?
Presi-dentures!

What always sleeps with her shoes on?
A horse!

A man went out in pouring rain and forgot his umbrella, yet his hair didn't get wet. How?
He was bald!

Which dog has no tail?
A hotdog!

What has no beginning, middle or end?
A doughnut!

What runs all day but never moves?
Your refrigerator!

What flies all day but doesn't move far?
A flag!

What has a bark but doesn't bite?
A tree!

What type of dress can never be worn?
Your address!

What gets smaller the more you put in it?
A hole in the ground!

What asks but never answers?
An owl!

Why do cows look up at the night sky?
To star-graze!

What has 4 legs but never runs?
A table!

What gets whiter the dirtier it gets?
A chalkboard!

Which animal has a secret name?
The anony-moose!

What is there more of the less you see?
Darkness!

Funny Tongue Twisters!

Tongue Twisters are great fun!
Start off slow.
How fast can you go?

Sharp smart shark.
Sharp smart shark.
Sharp smart shark.

Extinct insects.
Extinct insects.
Extinct insects.

Six slowly sliding slippery snails.
Six slowly sliding slippery snails.
Six slowly sliding slippery snails.

Stu chews Stu's shoes.
Stu chews Stu's shoes.
Stu chews Stu's shoes.

Chip shop chips.
Chip shop chips.
Chip shop chips.

Blue burger burglar.
Blue burger burglar.
Blue burger burglar.

Frogs feet flash.
Frogs feet flash.
Frogs feet flash.

Tommy Tucker tried ties.
Tommy Tucker tried ties.
Tommy Tucker tried ties.

Grey goats graze.
Grey goats graze.
Grey goats graze.

Mrs Smith's fish sauce shop.
Mrs Smith's fish sauce shop.
Mrs Smith's fish sauce shop.

Fred threw fast throws.
Fred threw fast throws.
Fred threw fast throws.

Free fleas flew.
Free fleas flew.
Free fleas flew.

Sheena leads, Sheila needs.
Sheena leads, Sheila needs.
Sheena leads, Sheila needs.

Big blue box of biscuits.
Big blue box of biscuits.
Big blue box of biscuits.

Seth sells thick socks.
Seth sells thick socks.
Seth sells thick socks.

Black back bat.
Black back bat.
Black back bat.

Which witch wished which wicked wish?
Which witch wished which wicked wish?
Which witch wished which wicked wish?

Creepy crabs clammer.
Creepy crabs clammer.
Creepy crabs clammer.

Willy's really weary.
Willy's really weary.
Willy's really weary.

Green glass globes.
Green glass globes.
Green glass globes.

Six slippery snails slide.
Six slippery snails slide.
Six slippery snails slide.

Funny fluffy feathers.
Funny fluffy feathers.
Funny fluffy feathers.

Pack black pens.
Pack black pens.
Pack black pens.

Bonus Funny Jokes!

Why didn't the girl want to kiss the vampire?

It's such a pain in the neck!

Which elf sang the best songs?

Elf-is Presley!

Where do chickens go for a laugh?

The funny farm!

Why did the book go to the chiropractor?
To get her spine adjusted!

What time is it when an elephant sits on your lunch box?
Time to get a new lunch box!

What did the poodle say to the flea?
Stop bugging me!

What washes up on really, really small beaches?

Microwaves!

What happened when the cleaner slipped on the floor?

He kicked the bucket!

What goes up if the rain comes down?

An umbrella!

What do volcanoes eat for a snack?
A Lava-cado!

What do you call a grumpy cow?
MOOOO-dy!

What starts with gas but only has 3 letters?
A car!

How do you get a one armed boy out of a tree?

Wave at him!

Why did the thermometer go to college?

To get more degrees!

What kind of paper likes singing?

Wrapping paper!

What is white and black and eats like a horse?

A zebra!

What do garbage trucks eat for lunch?

Junk Food!

Why did the tissue dance all night long?

It was full of boogey!

What did the really sleepy man read?
The snooze paper!

What do you call a girl who loves honey?
Bea!

How did the artist cross the river?
He used the drawbridge!

Why did the chef spend 10 years in jail?
He beat the eggs and whipped the cream!

What is the easiest way to make a hot dog stand?
Steal its chair!

What did the taxi driver say when he couldn't find his taxi?
Where is my taxi?

Why did the boy put 3 pieces of candy under his pillow?

So he could have sweet dreams!

What do you get treated for if a computer has bitten you?

A Megabyte!

Why did the coin collectors have lunch together?

For old dimes sake!

What do you do with a dog that chases kids on a bicycle?

Take away his bicycle!

How did the butcher introduce his new girlfriend to his family?

Meet Patty!

Why did the artist never win at any sports?

He kept on drawing!

Why was the Mexican restaurant so popular?

It was the taco the town!

What happened to the owl that lost his voice?

He just didn't give a hoot!

Why was the mommy kangaroo sad when it rained?

The kids had to play inside!

Where do the friendly horses live?
In your neigh-borhood!

Which dinosaur knew more words than some humans?
The Thesaurus!

What game to mice play?
Hide and squeak!

Bonus

Knock Knock Jokes!

Knock knock.

Who's there?

Harry.

Harry who?

Harry up! It's time to go!

Knock knock.

Who's there?

Ooze.

Ooze who?

Ooze in charge here my good sir?

Knock knock.

Who's there?

Amos.

Amos who?

Amos quito ZZZZZZZZZZZZ!!

Knock knock.

Who's there?

Olive.

Olive who?

Olive here but I forgot my key!

Knock knock.

Who's there?

Walnut.

Walnut who?

I walnut leave without you!

Knock knock.

Who's there?

Ben.

Ben who?

Ben meaning to call in for ages!

How have you been?

Knock knock.

Who's there?

Alison.

Alison who?

Alison to music all day long because I love it!

Knock knock.

Who's there?

Yorkies.

Yorkies who?

Yorkies are needed to open this door!

Knock knock.

Who's there?

Don.

Don who?

Don ya want to open the door before I freeze to death!

Knock knock.

Who's there?

Avenue.

Avenue who?

Avenue seen the news!

Quick! Let's go!

Knock knock.

Who's there?

Alby.

Alby who?

Alby back in a minute, so just wait there please!

Knock knock.

Who's there?

Freddy.

Freddy who?

Freddy set, go! I'll race you to the letterbox!

Knock knock.

Who's there?

Sam.

Sam who?

Sam day I will remember my key and then I won't have to knock!

Knock knock.

Who's there?

Early Tibet.

Early Tibet who?

Early Tibet and early to rise!

Knock knock.

Who's there?

Waiter.

Waiter who?

Waiter I finish telling all these jokes!

Then I'll tell you some more!

Knock knock.

Who's there?

Says.

Says who?

Says me, that's who! Ha Ha!

Knock knock.

Who's there?

Icing.

Icing who?

Icing so loud I need earplugs!

Knock knock.

Who's there?

Yvette.

Yvette who?

Yvette helps sick animals get better!

Knock knock.

Who's there?

Razor.

Razor who?

Razor hands in the air like you just don't care!

Knock knock.

Who's there?

Henrietta.

Henrietta who?

Henrietta too mucha spaghetti!

Knock knock.

Who's there?

Greta.

Greta who?

Greta move on! We have to go!

Knock knock.

Who's there?

Kenya.

Kenya who?

Kenya keep the noise down please!

I'm trying to sleep!

Knock knock.

Who's there?

Robin.

Robin who?

He's Robin your house!

Call the Police!

Knock knock.

Who's there?

Dwayne.

Dwayne who?

Dwayne the pool quickly!

I think Billy Bob fell in!

Thank you so much

For reading our book.

I hope you have enjoyed these funny jokes for 10 year old kids as much as my kids and I did as we were putting this book together.

We really had a lot of fun and laughter creating and compiling this book and we really appreciate you for reading our book.

If you could possibly let us know what you thought of our book by way of a review we would really appreciate it 😊

To see all our latest books or leave a review just go to
kidsjokebooks.com
Once again, thanks so much for reading.

All the best,
Jimmy Jones
And also Ella & Alex (the kids)
And even Obi (the dog – he's very cute!)

Made in the USA
Middletown, DE
07 August 2020

14679884R00066